Free the lines

clayton junior

This paperback edition published in 2018.
First published in hardback in 2016 by words & pictures,
an imprint of The Quarto Group.
The Old Brewery, 6 Blundell Street,
London N7 9BH, United Kingdom.
T (0)20 7700 6700 F (0)20 7700 8066
www.QuartoKnows.com

British Library Cataloguing in Publication Data available on request.

ISBN 978-1-91027-753-9

1 3 5 7 9 8 6 4 2

Printed in China

Free the lines

clayton junior

words & pictures

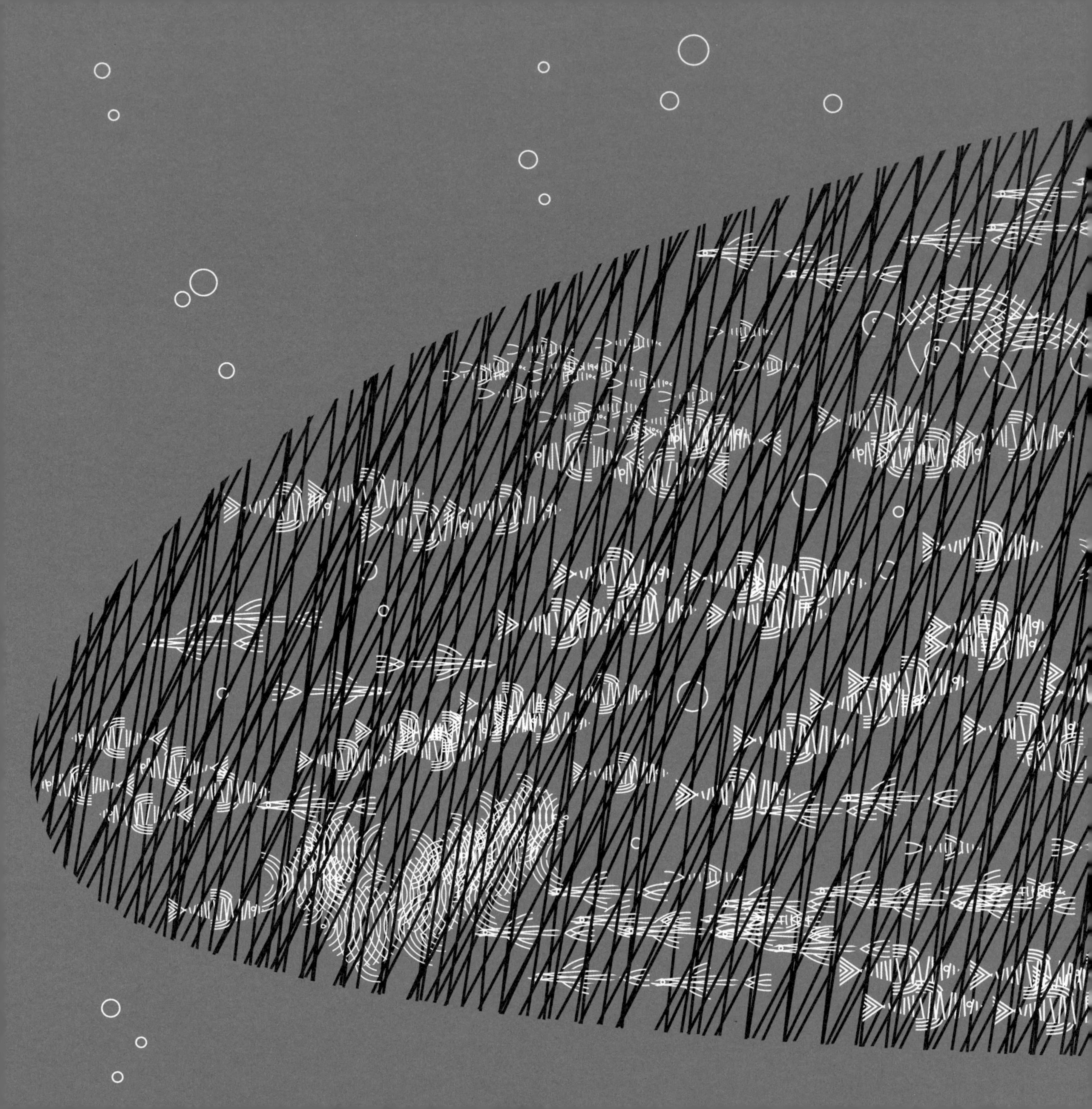

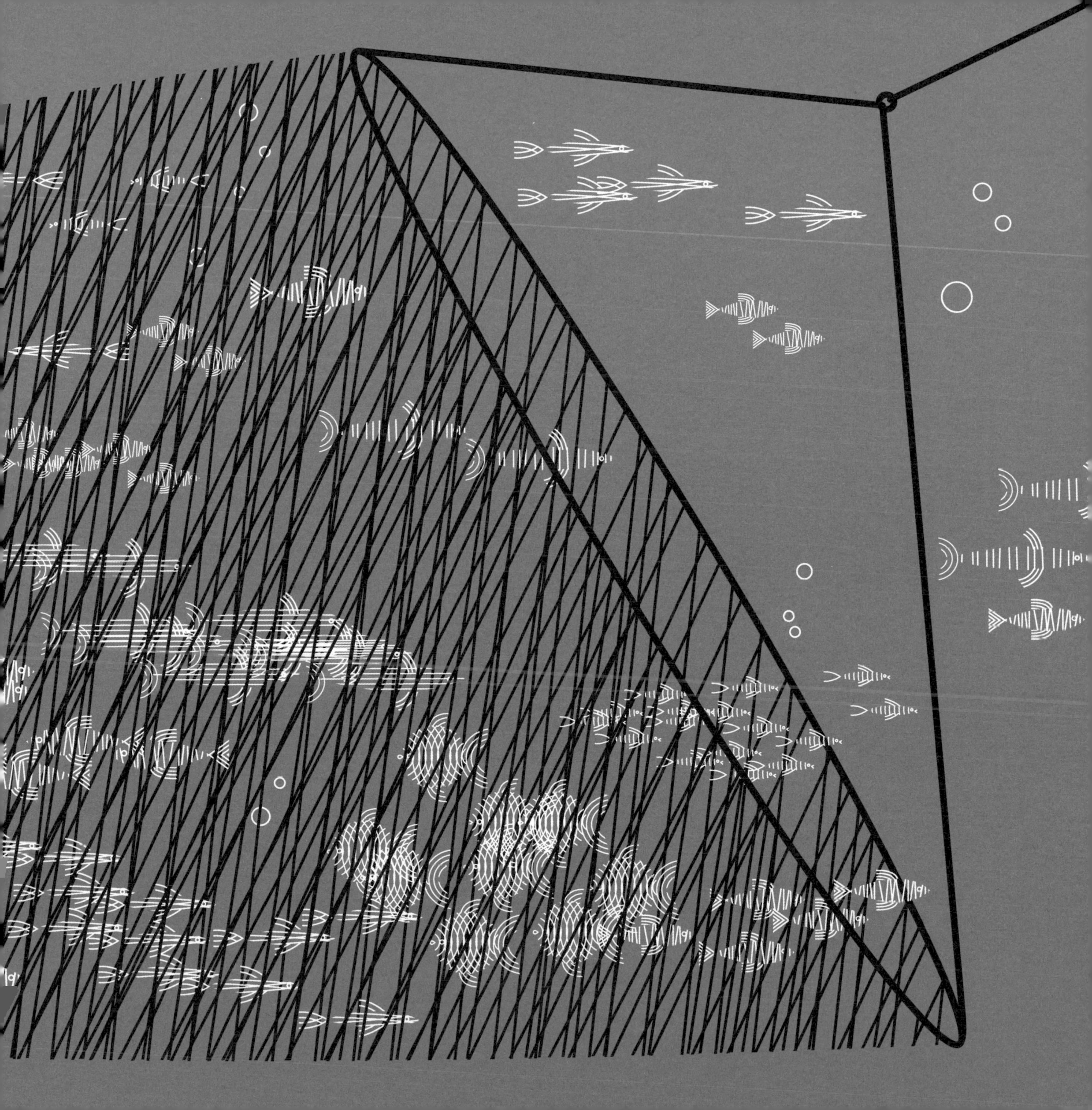

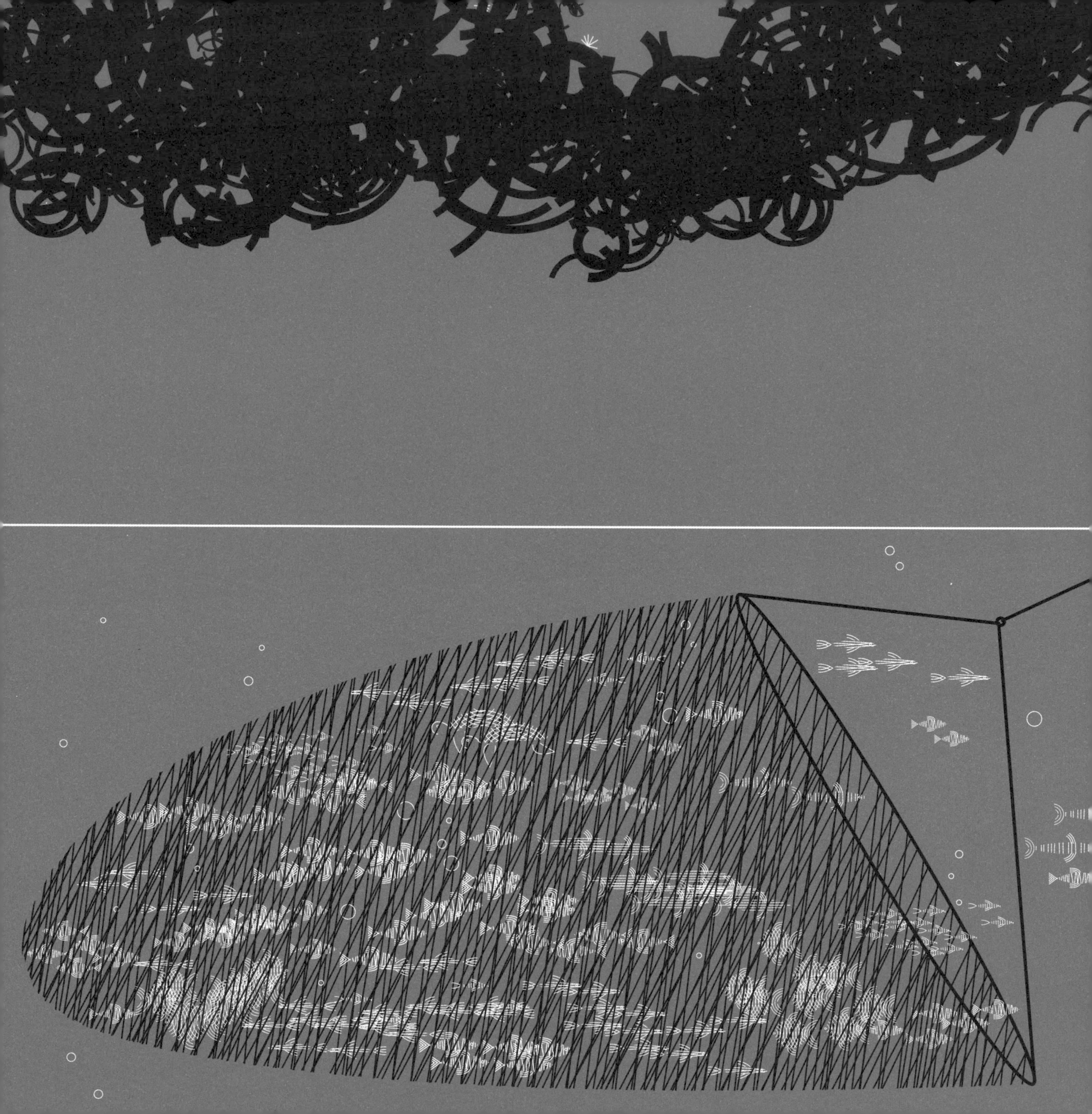